UNCLE SMOKE STORIES

ROGER WELSCH

UNCLE SMOKE STORIES

STORIES

NEHAWKA

TALES

OF

COYOTE

THE

TRICKSTER

ALFRED A. KNOPF

NEW YORK

THIS IS A BORZOI BOOK PUBLISHED BY ALFRED A. KNOPF, INC.

Library of Congress Cataloging-in-Publication Data

Welsch, Roger.
Uncle Smoke stories : Nehawka tales of Coyote
the Trickster / Roger Welsch.
p.   cm.
Summary: Uncle Smoke, a revered storyteller of the
fictional Nehawka tribe, shares four stories
about the legendary trickster, Coyote.
ISBN 0-679-85450-9 (trade)
[1. Coyote (Legendary character)—Juvenile fiction.
2. Coyote (Legendary character)—Fiction.
3. Indians of North America—Great Plains—Fiction.] I. Title
PZ7.W46849Un   1994
[Fic]—dc20   93-48309

Book design by Ann Bobco
Manufactured in the United States of America
10 9 8 7 6 5 4 3 2 1

For Jacinda Star

INTRODUCTION

I can remember the moment as if it happened yesterday—the moment I learned that the ways of Plains Indians are not fading memories of the past but a living part of modern America. It was over thirty years ago in Lincoln, Nebraska. I had studied anthropology in college, and had read almost every book I could find about the Omaha, Lakota, Pawnee, Oto, Ponca, and Mandan. The lives of these remarkable people fascinated me from the time I first began to read, and I was sorry that the Indians were long gone before my people even came to this country in the early part of the twentieth century. I regretted that I would never have the chance to see a Lakota Sun Dance, share the profound spiritual life of the Pawnee, or hear an Omaha Warrior Song.

I was talking with a friend about my feelings

one day, when he laughed and said, "But, Roger, all those things are still very much alive! I have many Indian friends and I go to their gatherings several times a year."

"The Sun Dance?!" I sputtered.

"Every summer," he said. "At Rosebud, South Dakota, on the Pine Ridge, at Wounded Knee…"

"But the Pawnee are gone and—"

"They are gone from Nebraska," Earl told me, "but the tribe is still strong, culturally and spiritually, in Oklahoma, and—"

"And the Omaha?"

"The Omaha still sing their tribal songs, still dance, still speak their native language, right here in Lincoln. They still…"

I could not hear enough. The most important thing Earl said was, "You know, Clyde Sheridan told me just the other day that the Lincoln Omaha will be having a Hand Game right here in town Saturday evening."

Earl gave me Mr. Sheridan's address and I drove immediately to his home. I was uncomfortable because I had never visited a Native American's home before. Besides, here I was, trying to barge my way into an event that, for all I knew, might be sacred, secret, and even forbidden to non-Indians. I told Mr. Sheridan about my interest in Omaha ways and that I wondered if I might attend the Hand Game—whatever that was—the next weekend.

I then learned my first lesson in the ways of the Omaha. Of course I would be welcome, Mr. Sheridan said. When Lewis and Clark came up the Missouri River, exploring the Louisiana Purchase in 1804, they learned the same lesson—the very foundation of Omaha culture is genuine hospitality. Here was something I had read about as a trivial piece of historical fact, and now I was experiencing the very same friendliness Lewis and Clark had found a century and a half before!

That was only the beginning. The next Saturday evening I made my way to the address Mr. Sheridan had given me. It was a run-down, dingy building in a seedy part of town, housing a used clothing store. Now I was really uncomfortable! I tried the door; it was locked. I peered through the dirty window; I could see nothing. By this time I was so uneasy that I was willing to turn on my heel and leave.

But then a door off to one side of the store

opened and three little children—dark-skinned *Indian* children—came running out. For the brief moment the door was open I could hear the throbbing of a drum and voices singing a kind of music I had never heard before. I went to the door and opened it. I peered down a long flight of stairs into a dark basement. The music pounded deep in the darkness. The three children ran past me again, laughing, and scrambled down the stairs. "Well," I thought, "if it's safe down there for children, it's probably okay for a big guy like me." I stepped down the long, steep stairs into the dark room full of strangers...and into a new life.

For four hours that evening I shared song and dance with these strangers who had every reason to wonder why I was intruding into their lives. They shared food with me, and laughter. I began to learn how to play the intricate Omaha Hand Game, a team guessing game a little like "Button, Button, Who's Got the Button?" but much more complicated. I made new friends. I learned that the Plains Indians are still very much a living culture. I found that I enjoyed the Omaha way of life. And most important, I discovered that these people—mostly very poor, generally neglected or

mistreated by mainstream white culture histori-
cally and even in the present—are warm, wonderful, wise people, from whom there is still a lot to
be learned.

Since that day I have tried to learn those lessons
from Native American friends and relatives—"relatives" now because I was adopted into the
Omaha Tribe in 1967 and was given the Wind
Clan name *Tenuga Gahi,* Bull Buffalo Chief. Even-
tually the people I met in that basement became
my best friends, my spiritual teachers.

Since that fateful night thirty years ago I have
learned a lot about Omaha, Pawnee, and Lakota
ways. The more I have learned, the more respect I
have gained for Native American people and traditional Native American ways. I sat at the Omaha
drum and worked at learning the old songs for ten
years. I met elders and listened to their stories
from history and folklore; I sat with the young
people and heard their complaints and aspira-
tions. I took sweats* and watched Sun Dances. I
danced at powwows and Gourd Dances. I have
prayed through many nights in tipis. I have been
blessed with cedar and sage. I have eaten fry
bread, corn soup, blue corn pudding, dog, buffalo,

---

* Explanations for many words dealing specifically with Native American and Nehawka ways
can be found in the Glossary beginning on page 75.

and wasna. My life has been changed for the better by the power, honesty, warmth, and humor of my Native American friends. In their wisdom, they knew all about my life in middle-class America, but I knew nothing of their rich and wonderful culture, which they generously shared with me.

I would not for a moment want to mislead you about Native Americans in the United States today, however! At powwows and ceremonials you can see them in feathers, beads, and bells, whirling the old dances and chanting the old songs, it is true. But during the rest of the year you are much more likely to find Ojibwas, Modocs, Navajos, Cheyennes, or Omahas working in the stock market in three-piece suits, farming in overalls, dancing with the ballet in tutus, buying groceries in jeans and sweatshirts, or opening a locker next to yours in your school. They speak English and drive cars and trucks. Native Americans run for Congress, become boxing champions, write books, teach classes, and run businesses.

All of us, after all, are something—Irish, German, Japanese, Mexican, Lao, Afghan. Sometimes (especially in the United States!) we are a lot of things. And sometimes we are lucky enough that our grandparents and parents have remembered and passed along to us the ways of our ancestors, our origins, our *roots*. I was born to a German family and so we always ate a few German foods on festive occasions and my father still tells me an occasional German proverb. We are still "German," yet it would not be easy to identify us as Germans as we go about our daily lives.

Native Americans are exactly the same. Some tribes have remained very strong (in part because they were often isolated on reservations, in part because their culture is strong and beloved to them and they do not want to lose it); others have weakened and even disappeared. Some Omahas cherish and try to remember the old ways; some are embarrassed by them and want to forget them. Some tribes keep their beliefs to themselves, a sacred secret; others are happy to share the magnificence of their culture with outsiders. In many cases, Native Americans are uneasy about letting others know their customs.

You can't blame them. The experience of many tribes with mainstream American culture has not been a happy one. Television and movies have all too often shown Indians as blood-crazy murderers, attacking innocent settlers and ranchers. Many tribes have lost their land and language to the white man. Many were ravaged by the white man's diseases. Some tribes have been wiped off the face of the earth. The Omaha, the people I know best, were farmers. They lived in permanent villages of large sod houses very much as the white homesteaders would later. They went on occasional buffalo hunts for meat and hides, but most of the time they tended their fields of beans, corn, and squash along the west bank of the Missouri River in what is now Nebraska.

The Omaha welcomed French traders and trappers as friends and tolerated English soldiers and missionaries. They never fought a battle with the white man, ever. Today they are poor but very proud still living on the lands where they have been for four hundred years, a few hours north of the city of Omaha. Few are farmers today, but Omaha land is sacred to them because it has been theirs spiritually for centuries.

The Omaha Tribe is the historical foundation for the fictional Nehawka Tribe of Uncle Smoke. I invented the Nehawka Tribe for several reasons.

First, there are some interesting features of other tribes that I want to share with readers. By writing about the fictional Nehawka, I can include whatever cultural features I want, without leading the reader astray about the specific history of the Omaha or Pawnee or Ponca.

Second, there are many good, accurate descriptions of Omaha culture (and of Pawnee and Lakota culture)—some of them written by me! If you want precise, nonfictional information about the Omaha, you should turn to those studies. Here, however, I wanted to write some original stories which include information about Native American thought and culture *in the style of* traditional Native American tales. The fictional Nehawkas let me do all of those things. There was no tribe known as the Nehawka...but there is no reason why there couldn't have been!

Uncle Smoke's stories are the kinds of tales told by tribes all across the Plains, all across America. Today the Omaha do not tell many Coyote (or Rabbit) stories, but among other tribes such tales are very much alive. Just as Coyote is an animal, a man, a spirit, an idea—sometimes one, sometimes another, sometimes all four rolled into one—Coy-

ote stories are sometimes an amusement, sometimes a lesson, sometimes a religious mystery,
sometimes history. In some cultures Coyote stories can only be told at certain times of the year or
by certain people.

One Coyote story can be all of these things, de-
pending on who is telling the story and who is
hearing it. No *one* way of hearing a Coyote story is
"correct." A very young child might hear a Coyote
story and simply enjoy it as we enjoy an animated
cartoon; an older child might hear one of Uncle
Smoke's stories and come closer to understanding
why it is that people do the things they do; an
elder might hear the very same story and gain new
insights into the meaning of life and the sometimes confusing ways of The Great Mysterious—
just as some of us learn from the stories of the
Bible or the Koran.

In some tribes, the mysterious trickster the Nehawka know as Coyote is called Rabbit. In some
he is Spider. In modern Omaha stories, he is Mon-
key. Modern children—Native American and non-
Native American alike—know him as Bugs
Bunny, or the Road Runner, or Teenage Mutant
Ninja Turtles—part human, part animal, part
spirit; part fool, part genius, part hero, part foul-

up. When you think about it, that could be a description of just about any one of us, couldn't it? Perhaps that is what Coyote stories are—a way of looking at ourselves without looking too closely!

If you are anything like me, you will want to know more about the "Nehawka," the Omaha, Coyote, or the Plains. There are good books about all those things in your library. Better yet, find out about the Indian tribes that were and perhaps still are in your area. Go to museums and tribal culture centers to learn about them. Attend a powwow, or ceremonial. Find a Native American friend—in school, at a senior citizens' home, at work, or in the neighborhood.

Perhaps you too will find yourself some evening in an unfamiliar place, just as I did the evening I went to my first Omaha Hand Game, about to hear, see, and taste things you've never tried before. Perhaps like me you will discover another world, or even a new life, a new family, a new home. Perhaps you will find yourself in the Big Belly Lodge of the Nehawka.

THE FIRST FIRE

THE FIRST FIRE

ncle Smoke rattled the entrance flap of the Big Belly Lodge and peered into the dark interior. "It is getting cold," he announced. "If there is still room for me at the fire, I have news of Coyote."

"Come in, Uncle Smoke. Come in. Winter must surely be here," called Cottonwood. As an old woman from the south side of the Big Belly Lodge, she was in charge of the evening fire. "Did you bring your bowl? There is fat meat and fresh corn soup for you, if you brought your bowl and an appetite."

Uncle Smoke came into the great, round center of the lodge—the source of its name—and shook the cold from his shoulders. The twins, Badger Running and Blue, brought him a robe from their family's compartment in the lodge. They put it around his shoulders and led him to the honored position at the west side of the lodge's fire, facing the entryway. They had always loved Uncle Smoke, and they also knew that later this winter they would be asking for his advice. They would need him to compose new songs for their Young Woman Song rituals, when they would become women.

Cottonwood took his bowl and filled it with steaming corn soup and meat, carefully picking for him the most tender bits. Cottonwood felt a special affection for Uncle Smoke. Everyone in the village called him "Uncle," but he actually *was* Cottonwood's uncle—her mother's brother, and therefore a member of both her family and her clan.

Uncle Smoke ate slowly. Because it would be rude to rush him, everyone in the Big Belly Lodge tried to appear as if the evening were a normal one. Older children brought in wood and water for the morning fire. Men unrolled bedding in family compartments on the lodge's elevated platform. Children cleaned the dishes from the evening meal. Mothers groomed the youngest children and babies for the night. But no one went far from the lodge's door, or from the fire, because no one wanted to miss the opening lines of Uncle Smoke's story. That was surely why he had come this evening, as he had done every harvest season for as long as anyone could recall.

His intent, everyone knew, was to tell stories about that strange and powerful spirit Coyote for the entertainment and education of the children. But not just for the children. As Uncle Smoke himself often said, no one is too old to be reminded of the ways of Coyote. The Powers—all of those great spirits and forces that govern the ways of animals and man, the winds and rains—gave the Nehawka the stories of Coyote to tell and hear. So it was up to the Nehawka to tell those stories and to hear them. It was as simple as that.

Uncle Smoke carefully cleaned his bowl with the tuft of fragrant sweet grass handed to him by Badger Running and Blue. The activities of the lodge quieted in anticipation. Visitors from other lodges came quietly in, nodding to Cottonwood to seek her hospitality. She smiled and nodded in welcome to them all—Bad Eye, Milkweed Silk, little Sky Fire, With Stick and Turtle Heart from the Deer Lodge, Thumb and Lodge Mouse from the Crazy Dog Lodge, Elk Tooth and Wolf-Afraid-of-Him from the Sky Bundle Lodge.

Uncle Smoke pretended not to notice his growing audience. Everyone in the village knew that he loved these harvest evenings and the story-telling at the Big Belly Lodge, but it would have been impolite for him to boast of his skill. Tonight he would be the center of attention in the Turtle Creek Village of the Nehawka. He cleared his throat and looked around the lodge.

The eager eyes of all—from children who could barely crawl to toothless elders—were fixed on the fire. It would have been unfitting for a Nehawka to stare at the storyteller. All waited for his first words, the same words he said every harvest moon, the same lines that began every Nehawka Coyote tale: "Coyote lived with his blind grandmother in a lodge at the edge of a village."

Ah, the words were good, and softly, around the lodge, adults who were permitted to interrupt an elder muttered, "Uda, uda!" ("Good, good!")

Uncle Smoke looked about sternly. Sky Fire and With Stick giggled, and even Uncle Smoke couldn't help but smile a little.

"I will continue with my story of Coyote," he

said. "It's one you probably have heard before, and I'm sure it could be told better by someone else. But I shall tell it anyway." And he did.

UNCLE SMOKE'S TALE OF COYOTE THE HUNTER

One day Coyote said, "Grandmother, I feel that winter is coming. I am going to go out to hunt some meat for our drying racks."

"Oh, in the past you have not been a good grandson, but now you are growing into a good warrior and hunter! That is a welcome change!" she exclaimed. "Be sure to bring home plenty of meat. The muskrat lodges are very large already, a sure sign of a long, hard cold season."

Coyote took his bow and arrows, a lance, and a flint knife, and went west toward the buffalo grounds, hoping that the Thunderers would give him a fat animal with a deep, thick hide. When he got there, Coyote saw a fine young buffalo calf. Although the animal was only a year or so old, he was already large and had a thick coat even though winter was a full moon away.

Coyote looked at the calf and thought about

what good, tender meat and what a warm robe he would provide. But then he thought again. "If I take this calf now, I will only get what I see. If I wait until next year, he will be twice as large. Grandmother and I will have twice as much meat and a robe large enough for a tipi, moccasins, and even a parfleche or two, instead of only a bed robe." So Coyote went past the young bull and shot his arrow instead at an old crippled buffalo cow. He thought he was very wise for making this decision.

Coyote's grandmother complained all winter about the tough, stringy meat Coyote had brought for her to cook, and about the ragged, stiff robe she had managed to pry from the old buffalo cow, and about how hard it was for her old teeth to crack the marrow from the heavy bones. But as crabby as she could be, she was also grateful there was any meat at all. It was going to be a hard winter, and her grandson Coyote had not always done even *this* well. As much as he liked to boast about his skill as a hunter, more often than not hunger was a constant guest at the lodge of Coyote and his grandmother.

The next winter muskrat lodges were even

larger. During the night trees boomed as freezing sap split open their trunks and branches, even before the shortest day of the year. It was already a cold winter, but it promised to be worse before the cottonwood trees budded again. It would be a good year to have plenty of meat and warm robes safely stored in the lodge.

Unfortunately, this season Coyote's grandmother had even tougher meat and an even more pitiful robe than she had had the year before. When Coyote went hunting, he once again saw the same fine young bull—and this year he was much larger than last year. The bull had not fought with the large bulls of the herd, so his robe was still pretty and smooth. And he had obviously enjoyed good grazing because his ribs were well padded with fat.

Coyote looked at him and licked his lips, thinking about the full soup bowl he would have if he brought his grandmother this buffalo. But again he reconsidered. He thought how big that buffalo would be next year, with an even larger robe and much more meat. "No, I'll not be a fool and cheat myself," he said aloud.

So instead he found an old bull dying on the

prairie with two broken legs—perhaps the result of a fight with another bull, or a fall into a prairie dog hole. So there was meat for Coyote's grandmother to cook that winter, but it was tough and dry. She scolded that it was more suitable for moccasins than for the cooking pot. The old bull's hide was stiff and hairless; all she could make of it was four war shields, which she traded to some of the other women in the village for hides better suited for clothing.

The next fall, Coyote's grandmother waved her finger at him before he went out for the hunt. "This time bring us back some tender meat and a soft, thick robe," she said. "The Thunderers have not treated us well these past two years. Maybe they will be kinder this winter. But you must do your part too."

"Perhaps, Grandmother," Coyote said, and went out toward the plains where the buffalo grazed. Before he was even close to the herd, he spotted the grand bull buffalo he had seen the two previous hunting seasons. The bull was now taller than a man at the shoulder; his head was as big as the trunk on an old cottonwood tree.

The great bull buffalo let Coyote get close to

him, close enough to shoot an arrow. Coyote sat looking at the bull buffalo and thinking, "If he has grown this much in the two years I have been watching him, think what he will be like next year! I will save him for next winter. Then I will be able to invite friends in to sit by my fire, smoke, and eat tender meat. If I kill him now, I will rob myself and my grandmother of many parfleches of food. No, I know better than to gather my corn before it is ripe."

So, instead of taking the big bull, Coyote found some scattered parts of a stillborn buffalo calf. That winter Coyote's grandmother had to gather mice, frozen birds, dead fish, and whatever else she could find for her cooking pot. All the while she mumbled complaints about her no-good grandson. In the other lodges of the village everyone laughed at Coyote's foolishness.

It was a hard winter indeed for Coyote and his grandmother. Many times they considered how cruel the Thunderers had been to them. As you can imagine, they were glad when spring came and there was again food to be found. Coyote's grandmother never let him forget that the next autumn he would have to bring home plenty of good meat for her drying racks and a good robe for her bed. The last winter had almost killed her, she complained. This time he had to do a better job of hunting or she would die.

Coyote listened, but he smiled behind his lips because he remembered the great buffalo bull. He knew that this was the year he and his grandmother would enjoy its abundant meat and thick, warm coat.

When the winter hunting season came, Coyote left his grandmother's lodge and went again to the hunting ground. He could not, however, find the great bull buffalo he had been saving. Coyote circled the herd and asked other animals—Bear, Cougar, and Wolf—if they had seen his bull buffalo. They said they had not seen him this year. Finally, Coyote asked the eagle if, with his sharp eye, he had seen Coyote's buffalo. Eagle said, yes, he had seen the great bull. This year he was far to the west, on the hunting ground of the Pawnee.

"Oh no! That was my buffalo," Coyote wailed. "I have been saving that bull for this year! And the Thunderers have given him to the Pawnee?! Why are the Thunderers so cruel to me? I have done nothing to offend them!" He raised his face to the sky and cried piteously.

Eagle turned his head to one side and then the othcr, watching Coyote's curious performance. "What a fool you've been, Coyote!" Eagle said. "Three seasons in a row the Thunderers sent you and your grandmother the finest buffalo bull on the entire range. Three seasons in a row you rejected their gift and chose instead to chew on tough meat, to curl up in thin, hairless robes, and to hammer at stone-hard bones! This year the Thunderers had a council and decided to give the great bull to the Pawnee. At this very moment the Pawnee are having a thanksgiving feast, singing their gratitude to the Thunderers."

From that time on, in the winter Coyote has to eat bony mice, stillborn calves, old bulls, and tough cows, and whatever else other hunters leave behind. Sometimes late at night while he sits on his thin, stiff robe and gnaws on rock-hard bones, he thinks about the great bull buffalo he once could have had. He wonders how that meat would have tasted in his grandmother's cooking pot. He imagines what that thick, warm hide would have felt like on cold prairie nights. Many nights you can hear Coyote howling from the hills, complaining to the Thunderers about how badly they have treated him and his grandmother.

That hunting season, however, Coyote came back from his conversation with Eagle and had to face the worst trial of all—his grandmother's angry tongue. "Where have you been, you ugly, long-nose bush-tail?" she asked.

"Nowhere," said Coyote.

"And what have you been doing?" she asked.

"Nothing," he said.

"Uda, uda, Uncle," Smoke heard from around the fire as he finished his story.

"I hope you weren't hinting that we people of the Big Belly Lodge have nothing to offer our guests but mice and scraps," scolded Cottonwood. She handed Uncle Smoke two new moccasins richly decorated with porcupine quills and bulging with chokecherries, dried meat, and buffalo fat. "Here is something for you to take to your lodge with you, Uncle, so you won't have to starve like old Coyote and his grandmother."

"And some tobacco for your pipe, Uncle," said Cottonwood's husband, Cut-by-Flint, handing him a handsome pouch. "I hope our gifts are not so small that you go on the warpath tomorrow night instead of coming to tell us more about Coyote." Several laughed at Cut-by-Flint's good joke. Clearly Uncle Smoke's days on the warpath were over.

"If the young men insist that I go with them to strike coup against the Pawnee," said Uncle Smoke, smiling, "then how can I tell them no? Now, help me get up from this fire so I can go home. And perhaps one of these young braves"— he pointed to Thumb, who beamed with pride because no one had ever before referred to him as a brave—"will help me find my way back to my lodge without knocking down a drying rack or stepping on some sleeping dog."

THE SECOND FIRE

THE SECOND FIRE

On the following night those in the Big Belly Lodge were ready for Uncle Smoke. They had moved a good backrest and cushion to the position of honor on the side of the fire away from the door. Others in the lodge had joined Cottonwood in preparing a larger pot of supper than usual. There would be many more guests tonight, now that everyone in the village had heard that Uncle Smoke was telling stories about Coyote. All day the people of the Big Belly Lodge had been preparing gifts for him—a hairbrush made of corkscrew grass, a small clay pot of blue paint, and a bag of groundnuts, freshly stolen from a mouse nest.

Other lodges wished that Uncle Smoke would honor them with his stories, but Uncle Smoke told his stories only at the Big Belly Lodge. No one could remember why, or how it started, but it had always been that way. As far as anyone could imagine, it would always be that way, just as the ways of Coyote had always been the ways of Coyote.

If anything, the people of the other lodges were happy there was peace in the village and a welcome at the Big Belly Lodge. Though they might envy the Big Belly Lodge, they knew that they were lucky to be Nehawkas. They understood that Uncle Smoke's stories belonged to all of them. Ah, some of them wondered, what do you suppose the Kaduza or Pawnee do on nights like this? They probably have storytellers, but none like Uncle Smoke!

The sun went down, noticeably earlier than the evening before. The Nehawka of the Big Belly Lodge ate a good meal and began to prepare for the evening. Whatever pleasure there was to be tonight, all the usual tasks needed to be done early. No one wanted to be away gathering firewood or getting water from Turtle Creek when Uncle Smoke began.

So everyone in the Big Belly Lodge kept their hands busy, hoping the time until Uncle Smoke's visit would pass more quickly. Women worked at pounding wasna and sewing; men polished arrow shafts and twisted bowstrings; children played with dolls and toy horses. All watched and listened for Uncle Smoke's appearance at the lodge door flap.

But there was nothing.

"It is almost time to go to bed. I wonder if Uncle Smoke has gone on the warpath," growled Cottonwood, worried that her guest's supper was burning in the pot. The children of the Big Belly Lodge began to fuss.

"Perhaps I should go out and see if Uncle Smoke has gotten lost on his way to our lodge," said Cut-by-Flint.

"It would be better to ask someone from another lodge to check on him," Cottonwood said. She was subtly reminding her husband that a Nehawka lodge should not be so bold as to *expect* a guest, much less a gifted storyteller like Uncle Smoke. They could hope for a visit from him, but it was not the Nehawka way to expect him.

"Yes, I suppose... " But Cut-by-Flint was interrupted by a faint rattle at the flap, and Uncle Smoke's head poked through the entryway. "It is getting cold," Smoke said cheerily, as if he were not late at all. "If there is still room for me at the fire, I have news of Coyote."

Uncle Smoke should have known what to expect by now, since Cottonwood had played this game with him before—perhaps thirty times before— but still her words surprised him.

"We are all ready for bed, Uncle. The supper has been put away. The fire has been put to rest for the night. The children are all asleep. It has been a hard night because we had a talkative guest and... we...were...all...up...too...late...last...night."

"Ah, well, in that case I'll go back to my lodge and eat some scraps I saved from last night—" Uncle Smoke was interrupted by an outcry not at all typical of a Nehawka lodge where life was usually quiet and orderly. Children began to shout, "No, no, Uncle Smoke, come back! Don't leave until you give us a story about Coyote!" Cottonwood shouted, "What do you mean, 'scraps'?! Those were this summer's chokecherries and newly dried meat!"

Cut-by-Flint laughed. "Don't be offended by these people acting like those Kaduza savages on the other side of the Smokey River, Uncle Smoke!" he said. He leaped to Smoke's side and pulled him goodhumoredly toward his seat. "Here, oh honored Elder. Rest yourself." Cut-by-Flint swept his arms in mock formality. "I'm in charge here and I will beat anyone with a stick who does not show you proper respect." He waved a large stick of firewood around threateningly. Children squealed. Women laughed. "Don't you laugh, old woman," he said to Cottonwood. "Get this old warrior some food for his bowl. Surely we have some leftovers from our humble supper."

Cottonwood shook her sheephorn ladle at Cut-by-Flint to remind him that he should say such things only in jest; she took her hospitality and the prestige of the Big Belly Lodge very seriously. He looked briefly into her eyes, a liberty reserved for husbands and wives. She accepted his glance and then turned away, embarrassed that at his age he was still willing to show her that he loved her. She took Smoke's bowl and filled it generously.

"You have given our guest so much food, my wife, that now he will never get around to...to...talking with us," said Cut-by-Flint, not wanting to seem to expect a story.

"He is here to eat, not to talk," said Cottonwood.

One of the children in the lodge said quietly, "But everyone was sure that Uncle Smoke would be here to tell us another story tonight..."

Smoke turned and looked at the girl. "My child, don't you worry. They are just trying to confuse Coyote. Uncle Smoke can travel for days with an empty belly, but it is not easy to keep him quiet for long. Tonight there will be a story about Coyote. Perhaps we can let the old people like your parents go to sleep so it is just us youngsters sitting around the fire. Huh! That would be good."

"Uda," a small voice said, very much cheered.

"Yes, it is late," said Uncle Smoke. "I had a long journey to get here"—the door to Uncle Smoke's lodge was a stone's throw from the Big Belly Lodge—"and young girls delayed me with their flirting." He turned to Cottonwood. "This is good food and plenty of it, my niece, but perhaps I should take it home with me so I can begin my story. It is a long one and I want to finish before the sun comes up."

"No, Uncle. Take your seat. Fill your bowl. Eat. I promise that here we will not permit girls to bother you," laughed Cottonwood.

Smoke took his seat of honor and looked across the fire toward the children gathered near the entryway. "First, I have a riddle for you." The children leaned forward.

"Where do you live?" he asked. The children looked at each other in confusion; this question was too easy.

"I'll make a wager with you," said Smoke. "I will give an arrow to any of you who can tell me where you live." Uncle Smoke was well known for his fine arrows, so this was quite an offer. "And if you cannot tell me where you live, I will expect each of you to bring me five long, straight dogwood sticks so I can make arrows for our hunters and warriors."

The children now faced a real dilemma. As much as they wanted to win one of Smoke's arrows, should they lose, it might take each of them a full day to find five long, straight sticks of dogwood suitable for arrow making. While Smoke's question seemed easy enough, it was perhaps *too* easy.

"Quickly, quickly," Smoke laughed. "I want to get on with my story."

"Yes, yes, we will take the wager," the children finally said in one voice.

"Good. Then where do you live?"

"We live at Turtle Creek Village," they shouted in chorus.

"So, you say you live at Turtle Creek Village. It

would not be fair for one of us to judge whether or not that is the right answer, now, would it? So we will ask someone else to make the decision, someone whose wisdom we all respect. Ho, Grandfather Kill-Bear! Wake up and answer a question for us!"

Kill-Bear, the oldest man in the village, had been dozing on the earth bench behind Uncle Smoke. When he realized that he had been called on, he looked around in confusion. His daughter Otter Eye repeated Smoke's question and the children's answer.

Kill-Bear thought a moment, and then pronounced solemnly, "The young ones are wrong." There was a murmur of disbelief from the children. Smoke smiled in victory.

"We live at *New* Turtle Creek Village," said Kill-Bear. "The Smokey River swallowed the old village many years before I was born, many years before my great-grandfather was born. When I was a boy, I heard stories of the old village and how it was destroyed. It has been a long time since that story has been told. You know the story, Smoke. Perhaps you should tell it sometime soon."

"Good idea, Grandfather," Smoke said. Then he turned to young Goose Down, lying in her bed robe not far from where he sat. "Now, if I could just remember...At my age it seems harder for me to recall, exactly, where it was that Coyote lived... but I think it was with his six brothers..."

A chorus of children's voices sang out, by way of helping Uncle Smoke begin this evening's tale: "Coyote lived with his blind grandmother in a lodge at the edge of a village!"

"Yes, I believe you're right," said Uncle Smoke. "That's it. Coyote lived with his blind grandmother in a lodge at the edge of a village!"

COYOTE AND THE GREAT COUNCIL

And one morning, Smoke continued, Coyote's grandmother woke up to find he was already up out of his bed robes, combing his hair and washing his face. It was not often that Coyote was up before the sun was high in the sky, but it was even more unusual for him to comb his hair and wash his face. But there he was, and moreover, he was putting on his finest leggings and armbands.

"I don't know who you are," Coyote's grandmother joked, "but it appears that you have stolen my grandson's body as well as his clothing. You are a handsome young man and I want you to know that you are welcome to stay as long as you like."

"Grandmother," Coyote said seriously, "it is well enough for you to laugh, but I am on my way to a very important council."

"I don't know what mischief you're up to now," his grandmother said. "But if there is indeed going to be a serious council, I hope you will stay away. Let everyone go about their business without trouble from you. It is bad enough that you bring harm to yourself and your family. You should not bring trouble to strangers too."

"Grandmother, I have been invited to this council. The Smokey River has been chewing away at its sunset bank. Great chunks of land fall into the waters every day and disappear. Last spring the river took all of the Nehawkas' lowland cornfields, and it seems that within a few moons, probably yet this summer, the Smokey River will devour Turtle Creek Village. So, the two-legs, the four-legs, the winged creatures, the water animals, the insects, the Nunwack, all the spirits, and even the Thunderers are gathering to decide what is to be done. Everyone will be there."

"Well, then that would explain it. I suppose if

everyone is supposed to be there, then even *you* might be invited. I do wish that you would not go," she said. "Smokey River has been eating the land along its banks. It is dangerous to go there. I hope you know enough to stay away from its waters."

Of course Coyote ignored his grandmother, just as he always does, and headed toward Holy Hill, far above the Turtle Creek Village. On the way he passed along the banks of the Smokey River.

"Ho, brother Smokey River!" Coyote said. He could barely hear himself above the roar of the river's muddy water, which was now in full flood.

"Ho, yourself, Coyote. Can't you see I am busy today?" said the river.

"I thought I'd come down to wake you up. The sun is already above the hills and you are still in your bed." Coyote laughed at his own joke. But River did not seem amused: a huge piece of the bank, right at Coyote's feet, slid into the water and disappeared.

Startled, Coyote jumped back. "I am accustomed to seeing you come from upstream and move downstream," he said. "It is unusual for you to go sideways."

"I do what I will. I do what I must. I do what I

do," said River. "If you have business with me, get on with it. I have a good deal of work ahead of me yet today."

So Coyote sat down—at a safe distance from the edge of the water—and explained to the Smokey River that he was going to the Great Council. Some serious matters were going to be considered there. He, Coyote, had been invited because he was so important. He explained to River that he had composed a grand speech for the council; by way of practice, he gave his speech for River, complete with the gestures he had prepared for dramatic effect.

"Very nice," said the Smokey River. "*Very* nice."

Finally, already late, Coyote left River and set off for the Great Council. His path up Holy Hill was long and twisted. In fact, it took him one full day and night to reach the top. As he climbed higher and higher, Coyote could see how the river was moving ever closer to the Nehawka village and was indeed threatening to destroy all the lodges.

The Nehawka had built a huge arbor at the top of Holy Hill. A double circle of stout oak posts, covered over with leaf bows so those attending the meeting could sit comfortably in shade, it covered the entire summit. When Coyote reached the arbor, everyone else was already there. They were all waiting for Coyote.

"Ho, Coyote, our brother!" they called. "We were beginning to worry that you might not come to our council." The Thunderers, the Nunwack, representatives of all the earth's creatures, even the two-legs known as the Nehawka stood to greet him.

Well, thought Coyote, this is not the sort of greeting I usually get, but I like it and feel that it is long overdue. More often than not my cousins throw sticks and rocks at me or run to hide in their lodges so they don't have to talk with me.

"Yes, my brothers," he said. "I am glad you have called on me to be here. I think you will find that I have much wisdom to offer. I was late because I had important business to take care of."

It was not easy for all of the creatures and spirits to endure Coyote's rude tardiness and arrogant words, but the fact of the matter was that they did need him. In fact, they needed all the information and every idea they could find because their problem was not an easy one to solve.

Soon the great Nehawka drum in the center of the arbor began to boom as the Nehawka singers sang a special song they had composed for the occasion. It saluted all the Powers, and all the creatures of the earth, water, and sky, and told again of the Nehawka relationship to all those forces of life. The Nehawka still sing that song today. It is the harvest song that begins:

> *Hey! You Thunderers! Our great and*
> *powerful brothers!*
> *We welcome you to our lodge.*
> *Take this seat of honor,*
> *Warm yourselves at our fire,*
> *Fill your bowls,*
> *Join in our song.*
>
> *Hey! You Nunwack! Our great and*
> *powerful brothers!*
> *We welcome you to our lodge...*

The Nehawka singers even added a verse for Coyote. When the song ended, the Nehawka chief Scatters-His-Enemies presented his case to the Great Council. "My brothers and sisters, my allies and friends," he said, "thank you for following the long roads to the top of Holy Hill. We, the Nehawka, have been a good people. We have worked hard, fulfilled our spiritual obligations, cared well for the Sky Bundle. We have done our best to live a life of gratitude. It is not our way to ask anyone for help. We try to take care of ourselves. But now we must ask you, the great and powerful at this council, to help us. How can the village of our ancestors be saved from the deep and growling waters of the Smokey River?"

First, Badger spoke. "Perhaps Buffalo could have all his herds plunge into the river and change its direction with the bulk of their bodies."

"No," said Eagle. "I fear that the pounding of all those hooves on the way to the river's bank might only make the already shaking ground even more unsteady. Perhaps if all winged creatures simply drank their fill and flew away..."

Black Bear shook his head. "No," he said. "The water would simply come back the next day."

"Perhaps if the Thunderbirds no longer brought rain," said Crow, "the river would dry up..." Scatters-His-Enemies worried that if that should happen, Nehawka crops would dry up too and the people would starve.

Meanwhile Coyote sat quietly, thinking. He said nothing during the debate, which took the entire day. This was not like Coyote. Coyote always has something to say. Who can forget the time Coyote sat beside a tree and, seeing his tail sticking out of the other side of the trunk, argued with it for almost two days about who had the right to be there and who did not? This is the reason for the Nehawka saying, "He argues like Coyote, and Coyote argues with his own tail!" But this day, all day, Coyote was silent.

Finally, shortly after the sun went down, Beaver stepped forward with a new plan: "I will bring all my kin from the long banks of the Smokey and the many streams and rivers running into it. I will ask them to come to Turtle Creek and build dams and diversions along the sunset bank of the Smokey River to save the Nehawka village."

At last, here was a plan that made some sense! Scatters-His-Enemies said, "I think this may be a solution to our problem. Beaver, my brother, if you will do this for us, the Nehawka will forever honor you. Never again will we put your relatives into our cooking pots."

No one could think of any objection to Beaver's plan, so a vote was called for. Black Ant was appointed to count the votes. She went carefully around the crowded arbor, carrying her little white counting stones with her.

"Yes," said the four Thunderers with one voice. "Yes," said each of the Nunwack. "Yes," said Magpie and Crow, Red-tailed Hawk and Crane. "Yes," said Fish and Crawdad. "Yes," said Firefly and Mosquito. "Yes," said Sand, Grindstone, and Red Dirt. "Yes," said Mushroom and Cloud, Cottonwood, Milkweed, and Sweet Grass. "Yes," said Dog. "Yes," said Orphan. "Yes," said Drum, Moon, Turtle, Antelope, Snow, and Chokecherry. So the count went around, each of the creatures and spirits at the Great Council expressing approval for Beaver's plan.

"Yes," said Dogwood. "Yes," said Green Paint Stone. "Yes," said Rabbit. "Yes," said Turnip, Pumpkin, Rainbow, and Puffball. "Yes," said Rattlesnake.

"No," said Coyote.

Ant dropped her little white counters. The Thunderers snorted so loudly the arbor and all of Holy Hill shook. Those who had voted long before and were now napping were startled into wakefulness. No one could believe what they had just heard. All eyes were on Coyote. He repeated his vote, just in case someone had missed it: "No."

Coyote picked his teeth for a moment, even though he had not eaten for many days. He turned to his tail, as if expecting an argument. "I vote against Beaver's plan," he said. A few of the others at the council groaned and shook their heads. How fortunate that Coyote's one vote could not turn the overwhelming force of the majority!

"We have one vote—Coyote's—against the plan," said Black Ant.

"Not quite," said Coyote rudely. "Actually, I cast *two* votes against the plan."

"We each have one vote, Coyote," growled a Thunderer.

"I cast two votes against the plan," insisted Coyote.

"ONE vote against," growled all four of the Thunderers.

Very quietly—even Coyote knows better than to challenge a Thunderer!—*very* quietly, Coyote muttered, "Two votes against." The few who heard him paid no attention to his insolence.

Black Ant handed her two baskets of tallies to the Thunderers and Scatters-His-Enemies, who announced, "We have a clear vote for Beaver's plan. There is only one vote against the plan, and that is Coyote's."

A pipe of tobacco was passed around the arbor and everyone joined in smoking it to show their goodwill, to celebrate the success of the council, and to fortify themselves for the long trip home. All wished Beaver and his relatives well, except Coyote, who whispered to Beaver, "Two votes, and they are the only ones that count, my brother."

"Tell it to your tail," laughed Beaver, who was familiar with Coyote's troublesome ways.

Less than one full moon later, Coyote was sitting in the rain on a hill near the Turtle Creek Village. Orphan happened along and sat beside him. "Ho, Cousin," said Orphan.

"Ho, Cousin," said Coyote.

"It appears that our relatives, the Nehawka, are having some hard times down at the Turtle Creek Village."

"Or what's left of Turtle Creek Village," said Coyote. "The Smokey River had already eaten half the village by the time I got here this morning. I have watched two more lodges disappear into the flood since then."

"Whatever happened to Beaver and his people and their plan?" asked Orphan. He was having a hard time understanding the distress of the Nehawka over losing their homes, since he had never had one.

"For many sunrises Beaver's kin came to the Smokey and worked at their dams. But it didn't make much difference. River pushed aside their dams and diversions just as a windstorm tears apart the smoke of a campfire. If you look closely, over there where the big oak trees are piling up against the sunrise side of the river—no, farther upstream—you can see Beaver and some of his relatives clinging to brush and branches out in the river."

"So, Beaver's plan failed. I guess you were right when you voted against it."

Coyote thought about what Orphan said. "It was a good, honest council," he answered, "but there wasn't much I could do with only two votes."

"I've been meaning to ask you about that, Cousin," said Orphan. "Why did you insist on having two votes?"

"On my way to the council, I stopped and sought the advice of another, and he asked me to carry his vote to the council and cast it for him. So I did. My vote and his made two votes."

"Who did you visit? Whose vote did you cast?" asked Orphan.

Coyote pointed down at the Turtle Creek Village, where yet another lodge was sliding into the turbulent waters of the river. "I asked Smokey River," he said. "He told me that it was his intention to wash away the sunset bank all the way to the base of the valley. That, after all, is his nature. No matter how anyone else voted, Smokey River was going to take the Turtle Creek Village back. Actually, no one else's vote mattered. Not even mine."

Coyote and Orphan decided to get out of the rain, so they said their farewells and turned to take one last look into the valley of Turtle Creek just as the last Nehawka lodge fell into the river.

"Huh," said Orphan.

"Huh," said Coyote.

Later, Coyote returned to his grandmother's lodge. "Ho, Grandmother," he said.

"Ho, Grandson. Where have you been all day? What have you been doing?"

"Nowhere," Coyote said. "Nothing."

• • •

Without a word, Cut-by-Flint handed old Uncle Smoke a pipe he had tamped with tobacco and lit with an ember from the fire. Cottonwood brought him a small pot of water. Smoke puffed at the pipe and sipped at the water, but for a long time no one said a word or moved. In a Nehawka lodge one accorded a word or story a period of silence in keeping with its power.

"Uncle," said little Goose Down. "That is a very sad story. It brings tears to my eyes to think of our ancestors losing their village."

"Oh, no," laughed Uncle Smoke. "We cannot be sad about such things. They must happen and they do. It is the Nehawka way to learn how to live with those things that must happen."

"I still think it's sad," the small girl said.

"Now, now," scolded her mother, Brush. "It is not polite to argue with Uncle Smoke."

"Yes, little one," chuckled Smoke. "It's almost like arguing with Coyote."

"With Coyote?"

"Yes. I have *two* votes—my own vote and the past's vote. We cannot change the past any more than the Great Council could change the nature of the Smokey River. And think of this, little Goose

Down: are you comfortable here in the Big Belly Lodge? Do you like your bed, and this fireplace? And this corn soup and dried pumpkin? Isn't your mother's cooking all the better because her garden does so well here? Well, perhaps the best thing for the Nehawka was for the village to be moved here, up Turtle Creek and away from the dangerous waters of the Smokey River. Perhaps the Spirits of the Dead were only helping the Nehawka by destroying the old village. Although our ancestors did not understand at the time that they should be grateful, they were not suffering a disaster but were simply enjoying the help of greater and wiser Powers."

Again there was a long silence in the Big Belly Lodge. And then words of approval: "Uda!" "Uda, Uncle!" "Uda."

Finally, Uncle Smoke made an effort to rise. Many rushed to his aid. Gifts were pushed into his hand. Thumb rushed to his side, hoping that he would be accorded the honor of helping the grand old uncle back to his lodge again tonight.

"All you children! Don't forget to bring me the dogwood wands I have won in our wager. And you, Lodge Mouse," Uncle Smoke said, bringing honor to yet another young brave, "you can help me back to my lodge tonight too. And don't you head out on the warpath, or take out your love flutes, without including me in your party!"

"Turtle Heart, With Stick, help our uncle with his gifts," said Cut-by-Flint. "Hey, Uncle, Cottonwood is thinking of cooking more pumpkin tomorrow night, with bone marrow. It will be good, seasoned with some salt Quick Bear just brought from down on the Sweet Water. If you know any other stories of Coyote, we hope to hear them. You are welcome always at the Big Belly fire, even without a story."

"I like pumpkin," said Uncle Smoke, looking over the full lodge he was leaving, "but I don't want to tell my stories unless there is someone to hear them." He turned and pushed through the lodge flap.

THE THIRD FIRE

THE THIRD FIRE

The following day Uncle Smoke came early to the Big Belly Lodge. He had done this before. To teach his Nehawka village the ways of Coyote, he liked to act as unpredictably as Coyote. Cottonwood had only gotten her evening fire going. The girls of the Big Belly Lodge had just left to get water from the creek. In fact, Cottonwood, a few elders, and some mothers with babies were the only ones still in the lodge. The sun had just gone down when there was a rustle at the lodge door skin. Smoke stuck in his head and said, "It is getting cold. If there is still room for me at the fire, I have news of Coyote."

"There is no one here to listen to your stories and no food on the fire," said Cottonwood to her old relative, "but why don't you come in and warm yourself by our fire anyway, Uncle? There will be

45

pumpkin and marrow fat later. Maybe someone will come in who is willing to waste some time listening to your stories."

"Perhaps," snorted Smoke, admiring his niece's skill in dealing with his irascible ways. Cottonwood helped him to the seat of honor and brought him a cup of water. "Badger Running and Blue," she called, as soon as her two daughters returned from the creek, "your Uncle Smoke is here. I know he will want to help you in a few moons with your Young Woman Song rituals. Maybe you should comb his hair for him and get out all the cockleburs and ticks."

Cottonwood knew that as a good Nehawka her uncle had had his two baths that day and had taken care in grooming himself for his performance tonight. He had spent the afternoon in his sweat lodge, cleansing his body and his mind in preparation for recalling and recounting Coyote's adventures. He had rubbed himself with sage. He had rinsed his mouth with mint tea and brushed his few remaining teeth with a willow-twig brush. Her suggestion that he might have cockleburs and ticks in his hair was so outrageous, he knew at once it was a joke.

Smoke turned to Cottonwood in mock anger.

"Well, at least you could help this old warrior look handsome for his audience tonight. Blue, take some of the sunflower oil from the small pot in my compartment and comb it through this warrior's hair. But don't make him look too good or all the young girls in the village will be flirting with him again tonight."

As the people of the Big Belly Lodge came in, they were surprised to find old Uncle Smoke already sitting in his chair, smoking some of Cut-by-Flint's tobacco, being groomed by his great-nieces. They said nothing because there was nothing to say. That too was the Nehawka way. They were glad to see the old gentleman in their lodge again that evening; they knew that he knew he was welcome. That was the way it should be among the Nehawka. They watched Cottonwood fill his bowl with his favorite treat, pumpkin, and watched him eat. That was the way it should be too: elders who had done so much to make the Nehawka strong should never go hungry.

It was good to know that some ways go on, that old stories and old storytellers were still honored. That's the way it was in a Nehawka lodge. The weather changed, the seasons changed, and names changed, but Nehawka ways did not change, and that was a comfort to everyone, the young and the old.

Uncle Smoke began, "Coyote was talking with his good friend Rabbit one day, when..."

A flurry of mumbling and complaint filled the lodge. Uncle Smoke stopped and looked around with mock surprise. "Do the Nehawka now interrupt an elder like the Kaduza? Whatever happened to the courtesy of a Nehawka lodge?"

"But Uncle Smoke...," Sky Fire said, stepping boldly forward to the old man's side. "You started the story wrong."

Smoke turned slowly, ominously toward the child. "I believe you are the one known as Pumpkinseed."

"Uncle Smoke, I am your great-granddaughter Sky Fire."

"Oh, yes, Sky Fire. Now I remember you. You are the one who spilled the soup bowl in my lap and on my best robe on the summer hunt last year. And now you are telling your Uncle Smoke, a Nehawka elder, a respected warrior, a caretaker of the Sky Bundle, an honored hunter, a noted storyteller, that he has made a mistake? Is that what you are saying, even though you are no bigger than a duckling?"

"Yes, Uncle."

"Then how do such stories begin?"

Sky Fire giggled because she knew that Uncle Smoke was only having fun with her. She drew herself up to her full height and spoke as loudly, as fully as she could, imitating her uncle's style: "Coyote lived with his blind grandmother in a lodge at the edge of a village..."

"Uda, uda!" said Smoke, embracing his great-granddaughter. "Uda. And so..."

SMOKE'S STORY OF COYOTE AND HIS SHADOW

Coyote lived with his blind grandmother in a lodge at the edge of a village. Coyote said, "Grandmother, I am going out to see what is going on."

"All I ask, Grandson, is that you not deal with that ugly split-mouth, long-eared Rabbit. He has been around the village lately, making trouble. We don't need trouble."

"Don't worry about me, Grandmother. I was thinking of...of...of going over by...by...by the river to...to...to catch some fish for supper."

"Well, that would be good," Coyote's grand-mother said, even though she could tell by his slow speech and rolling eyes that he was lying.

We all know what Coyote did, though, so I don't suppose I have to tell you. As fast as he could, he set about finding that unpleasant rascal Rabbit. And Rabbit was not hard to find: he had been thinking about that no-good troublemaker Coyote for a long time.

"Ho, Coyote, my beloved brother!" shouted Rabbit.

"Hey, Rabbit, my trusted friend!" cried Coyote.

"Coyote, I have been looking for you, my respected cousin. I have brought you a gift, this wonderful Day-Night Stone."

Coyote took the stone and rolled it over in his hand. "This is a very nice stone, my best friend. It is a shiny stone, and very round, and it has good weight to it. But why is it called a Day-Night Stone?"

"Because," Rabbit said sincerely, "it can turn day into night."

"How wonderful!" Coyote said. "I can see how this could be very helpful for me. How can I use it to turn day into night?"

"Simply close your eyes, hold the stone tightly,"

Rabbit said, "and say 'Turn day into night.'"

Coyote closed his eyes, clenched the rock, and said, "Turn day into night."

He stood there awhile and then opened his eyes. "It's still day."

"Well, now it is," said Rabbit. "But it was night when you had your eyes closed. Try it again."

Again Coyote closed his eyes and said, "Turn day into night." He waited a moment and then said to Rabbit, "Is it night?"

"Yes," Rabbit said. "It's so dark I can't even see you. Quick, open your eyes before something terrible happens to all of us!"

Coyote opened his eyes and Rabbit thanked him for ending the premature night. Coyote was impressed with this treasure Rabbit had given him.

"Say," said Rabbit. "Maybe you could do something for me, since I have given you such a fine gift."

"Uh, well," said Coyote uneasily, "what do you have in mind?"

"Nothing much," said Rabbit, eyeing the sky to the west. "I want your shadow, if you're not using it."

Coyote thought about Rabbit's offer for a while. It was true that he had not been using his shadow for some time. In fact, he couldn't recall ever using his shadow. "Yes, I will let you have my shadow, my dear relative," he said finally. "It seems like a small thing to give in exchange for the wonderful Day-Night Stone. Rabbit, my shadow is yours."

At that very moment, just as Rabbit had planned, a cloud passed over the two. Sure enough, Coyote's shadow disappeared. Coyote and Rabbit went their separate ways, both content with their new possessions. Coyote spent the afternoon holding his Day-Night Stone and closing his eyes to make night and opening them to restore the day. Rabbit spent his afternoon watching the sky and planning the next step in his trickery.

It was not long before Rabbit came back to Coyote. "Well," he said, "have you figured out yet how stupid you've been?"

"What?" said Coyote.

"I really tricked you this morning, and I am just wondering if you have figured out yet what a fool you've been."

"I...you...we?"

"Stupid Coyote, without your shadow, how are you going to know which way the wind is blowing?! How can you see if your hair is brushed? You numskull, now you are completely alone!

How will you make a buffalo surround all by yourself?! Who is going to give you advice, now that you don't have a shadow? Coyote, I can't believe how stupid you are. You have traded away your only friend."

Coyote was stunned by Rabbit's trickery. He sat on the hill for a full day, contemplating this terrible thing he had done. He imagined a life without knowing which way the wind was blowing, not knowing if his hair was brushed, never again tasting fresh buffalo meat, without advice, without a friend, with nothing. And the next day he set off on the run as fast as he could to find Rabbit. It was not long before Coyote came upon him, sitting under a tree.

"My dear, dear brother Rabbit, I want to talk with you about the loan I made to you of my shadow. It is time I had it back."

"It was not a loan. I gave you the Day-Night Stone and you gave me your shadow in return. It was a fair trade."

"I brought you the Day-Night Stone back."

"I don't want it back. I am content with your shadow. A shadow is no good to anyone in the night, so you don't need it. Since I have a shadow, I don't want night anymore."

"I…You…We…"

"I like your song, Coyote. I-You-We is a song I think you should be singing for a long time. I-You-We. Very nice."

"I want my shadow."

"What will you give me for it?"

"I will give you my courage."

Now, if there was one thing Rabbit wanted from Coyote, it was his courage, for in those days Coyote was a very brave fellow, even if he was also a little stupid.

"Yes," Rabbit said. "I will take your courage and give you back your shadow." Rabbit had cleverly watched the sky that day, watching for the clouds to clear away. They did, and there once again was Coyote's shadow, attached firmly to Coyote's feet.

Perhaps you already know something that Rabbit and Coyote learned only at that moment: No one can gain courage by taking it from another. Even though Rabbit took Coyote's courage away from him, he still has no courage of his own. He is still timid. And Coyote? He has no courage, because he gave it away.

So Rabbit went off with nothing to show for his day's conniving. And Coyote went home to his grandmother's lodge with his shadow intact but without his courage. When he got home, his grandmother asked, "Where have you been, you ugly, long-nose bush-tail?"

"Nowhere," said Coyote.

"And what have you been doing?" she asked.

"Nothing."

Uncle Smoke sipped at his water and puffed at the pipe Cut-by-Flint handed him. Thus he sat until the fire had died down to only a few embers. From the family compartments of Big Belly Lodge there were sounds of snoring and heavy breathing. Still Smoke and many of his listeners sat looking into the fire, thinking about the manipulations of Coyote and Rabbit.

"Father," a child said in one of the darkened compartments, "Uncle Smoke told a story about Coyote knowing so much last night, but tonight he is a fool like the puppy we had last summer."

"Shhh. Coyote is like that."

"Why can't he just make himself brave, like a Nehawka warrior?"

"Perhaps he can. That is not something for us to know. What we do know is that Coyote is like that."

"Is the Coyote in Uncle Smoke's stories the coyote we see on the hills and hear at night? Or is he a spirit like the Thunderers? Or a man like you, Father?"

"Shhh. Coyote is like that. He is all those things. Like you, little one, like you."

Finally Smoke made a motion to rise, and many in the lodge rose to help him. Again young warriors helped him to the door and across the village to his lodge. Others carried the gifts he had received from the grateful people of the Nehawka village.

The next day the sun shone brightly in the cold Plains sky. The Nehawka village was unusually quiet. It was as if Coyote and Rabbit, their ways and adventures, were still in the eyes and ears of the Nehawka. All day, except when he was taking his sweat in preparation for the fourth night's story, Smoke sat on the south side of his lodge, in the sun. Quietly, thoughtfully, he noted the effects of his narrative. He spoke to no one, but Cut-by-Flint saw him admire his shadow and nod several times, all the while saying, "Uda, uda."

THE FOURTH FIRE

THE FOURTH FIRE

That evening Uncle Smoke came to the Big Belly Lodge solemnly. As expected, he shook the lodge's door flap and repeated his traditional greeting: "It is getting cold. If there is still room for me at the fire, I have news of Coyote." While everyone was again happy to see Smoke, there was also some sorrow, because this would be the last of his stories, probably for some moons. As with everything in the Nehawka world—the seasons, the Thunderers, stages of life for a Nehawka, songs for sacred bundles and blessing—Uncle Smoke's stories came to them in sets of four.

Uncle Smoke went to his seat on the far side of the lodge fire and Cottonwood brought him food for his bowl. Cut-by-Flint brought him a pipe of tobacco. Others slipped him gifts or announced that later this winter they would have a new robe for him. One warrior promised Uncle Smoke a full side of fresh buffalo ribs, should the hunt go well.

Then his listeners settled down in their robes to listen. This night, the last of the traditional four, Smoke took his time eating. That was fine with his friends and relatives. They were happy to have this night go on as long as possible.

Smoke finished his meal, sipped at his water, and began the prayer that marked the fourth and final story. He offered water, meat, and tobacco to the four poles of the lodge. Then he thanked the Powers, the Thunderers, Coyote, and the Great Mysterious. He prayed for his family, his lodge, his clan, his people, the land, the sky, and all the gifts he enjoyed as a Nehawka—their good kin and allies, their lodges and village, the year's good harvest, all of the stories they had given the Nehawka people to tell and hear.

He drew a deep breath and looked around the Big Belly Lodge, as if he were sorting through all the stories in his mind for just the right one for this occasion. Again he drew a breath, and then began.

• • •

THE STORY OF COYOTE'S COURTSHIP

oyote lived with his blind grandmother in a lodge at the edge of a village. One day he said, "Grandmother, I am a young man and warrior. It is time for me to put on my finest clothing to court and win a wife."

"I have dreaded this moment for many years," Coyote's grandmother cried. "Who would have an ugly, lazy, foolish scruff-tail like you? Only another ugly, lazy, foolish scruff-tail, that's who! And then there will be three of us starving in this cold lodge. You should use your energy more wisely, to find some food and firewood for your household. Why don't you kill a buffalo for our drying racks, and for moccasins? You are going on a foolish errand. Now, whatever you do, do not go to that Nehawka village by Turtle Creek. The women there are too beautiful for a miserable creature like you, and the Nehawka warriors are too strong."

Of course, we all know what Coyote did as soon as he was out of sight of his grandmother's lodge. He headed directly for the village of the Turtle Creek Nehawka. As is proper, Coyote began to

sing his greeting song when he was still well outside of arrow shot of the Nehawka lodges, so no
one would mistake him for an approaching
enemy. Everyone in the village turned to see who
was about to visit them. Women began to prepare
food for a guest. Men sang a welcoming song, as is
usual among the Nehawka.

The Nehawkas' songs and words of welcome
turned to laughter when they saw who it was they
were greeting. "It is only Coyote, and look at him.
His clothes are even more filthy than usual. His
hair is uncombed. He limps along on his bad leg.
His tongue is hanging out of the side of his mouth
and is covered with dirt from his travels. His ribs
show. Hey, Yellow-Eyes, why have you come to
honor the Turtle Creek Village?! Have you come to
organize a war party against the Kaduza across the
Smokey River? Or are you off on an adventure to
pluck a tail feather from the Thunderbirds?!"

Everyone knew, of course, that Coyote brought
no honor with him. He didn't have the courage or
strength to pull a feather from the tail of a prairie
chicken, let alone a Thunderbird.

The closer Coyote came to the village, the more
the Nehawka could see of his poor clothing and

ugly face, and the louder their insults grew. "Hey, Tail-Between-Your-Legs, have you come to sing us more of your fine songs, or tell us stories of your bravery? Ha, Coyote! Snoring is a prettier sound than your songs! You have no bravery, so you have no stories!"

Coyote entered the center of the village, among the lodges, and when the laughter finally died down, he rose to his full height and announced, "Yes, I am here for all that." Again his voice was drowned out by Nehawka laughter. "But most of all..." he paused until the voices fell quiet again. "But most of all, I have come to court myself a Nehawka wife."

The villagers laughed as they had never laughed before. Coyote! Come to the Turtle Creek Village to court! To take a Nehawka woman as a bride! Could anything be more foolish? This time Coyote had outdone even himself!

"Yes!" shouted Full Quiver, moving quickly to Coyote's side. The Turtle Creek villagers knew that Full Quiver was always ready for a joke. They knew Full Quiver would give them plenty of laughter in his dealings with Coyote. "I shall be your ally in your courtship, old friend. I am the finest hunter in the Turtle Creek Village"—there was a cheer from the villagers by way of affirming Full Quiver's boast—"and you and I shall go out with some of the other sure-eyed hunters to get food for your wedding feast."

With exaggerated pomp a dozen young hunters grabbed their bows and arrows and marched out of the village, laughing and singing. Coyote strutted in the middle of them with his splintering bow and crooked willow arrows. They had not gone far when a jackrabbit sprang from the plum brush and set off across the countryside in a wild, erratic dash.

"No, comrades, no sense in trying to shoot him," shouted Full Quiver. "No one can hit Jackrabbit with an arrow unless it is blessed by the Thunderers."

But Coyote pulled a crooked arrow from his ragged quiver. He set it to the often-repaired string of his broken bow and let it fly in the general direction of the fleeing jackrabbit. Coyote's crooked arrow flew a crooked path, up and down, back and forth, in exactly the same way that jackrabbit runs. As the jackrabbit disappeared over the hill, Coyote's arrow caught him right between his shoulders.

"Well, that wasn't so hard," said Coyote, picking up his kill. "It's only a matter of using well what you have."

As the small band of hunters could no longer laugh at Coyote's hunting skills, they were a good deal quieter. Before long, they smelled the smoke of a campfire. "The wind is not blowing from Turtle Creek," said Full Quiver uneasily. "This smoke comes from the direction of the Kaduza villages. We may have stumbled on a Kaduza war party. You, Red Fox and Gizzard, creep along below the hill that way. See what you can see. Juniper and Kills-Enemy, go along the creek bottom. You others, come with me and we will sneak up along these chokecherry bushes to see if we can spot the camp from the other direction."

"What about me?" asked Coyote.

"You stay here. The Kaduza are fierce enemies and even if this is only a small raiding party, fighting them will be a task for real warriors. If it is a large war party, we may need to flee to the village. If we have time, we may need to get more braves." And the three small attack parties crept off quickly and quietly to survey the situation.

Crawling well below the horizon, lying within the bushes and tall grasses, the Nehawka peeked over the brow of the hill. What they saw chilled them. There were many Kaduza warriors in the camp below them—far too many for Full Quiver's small hunting band. The Kaduza were preparing themselves for war. They were moving much too quickly for any of the Nehawka warriors to return to the Turtle Creek Village with a warning.

The Nehawka braves tried and tried to think of what they could do, other than a simple suicide attack on the Kaduza. Such a tactic could only delay a little the inevitable slaughter of the people of Turtle Creek.

There was no need for Full Quiver and his men to think or worry, however, because Coyote had also been thinking and worrying. Back where his comrades had left him, Coyote thought about what sort of bride he would choose when they returned to the village. He imagined how he would devise a new dance to show everyone how he had slain the jackrabbit with a single arrow. He began to compose a fine new song to celebrate his successful hunt. Oh yes, with his jackrabbit for the feast, his new dance and beautiful song, he would impress the girls of Turtle Creek Village! He would have the prettiest of the Nehawka girls for his bride.

The more Coyote thought about the feast, song, dance, and his new wife, the more excited he became. About the time Full Quiver and his men were contemplating their war plans, Coyotc was carried away with thoughts of his triumphs. He sprang to his feet and began to dance and sing wildly on the very top of the hill, in full view of the Kaduza war party. He waved his broken bow and crooked arrows as he rehearsed his reenactment of his hunting victory. As loud as he could, he sang his new song:

> *I-you-we!*
> *I slay him with one arrow,*
> *He who crosses my path.*
> *I-you-we!*
> *There is no escape, you rabbits;*
> *Sing your death songs,*
> *It is a good time for you to die.*
> *I-you-we!*

The astonished Kaduza warriors stared up at Coyote's crazy dance on the hill above them. "He is not afraid of us," cried one of them, "even though we are so many. He must have many allies with him."

"He sings of killing us, each with one arrow. He must be a very brave warrior," shouted another, dropping his own weapons and starting a quick retreat. "He calls us 'rabbits.' Although he is small and his weapons are ragged, he must be like a grizzly bear in battle." And within a moment the Kaduza were in full flight, leaving behind all of their weapons and supplies.

"Hmm," said Coyote, watching the fleeing warriors. "Maybe my dance and song still need a little practice. In the meantime, we can return to the village and take along all these things for safekeeping for our Kaduza friends."

Coyote gathered up the Kaduza moccasins filled with dried meat, and their abandoned bows and arrows, war axes, clubs, and spears. He took the shields and medicine bundles and parfleches of food, calling to Full Quiver and his companions to help him. "Hey, comrades! Come help me. I cannot carry all these things by myself!" he shouted.

"I have never seen such a fierce warrior," stuttered Full Quiver, helping Coyote gather up his booty.

"It's all a matter of knowing your enemy," said Coyote, smiling.

When the hunting party returned to Turtle Creek, the villagers were astonished to see all the Kaduza goods the hunters had brought back—food, clothing, and weapons. Everyone wanted to hear how this had happened—especially why Full Quiver and his kinsmen were no longer laughing at Coyote.

"Tell us about your hunt and the victory over the Kaduza!" everyone in the village shouted. "Let us have a feast, and music, and dance, so you can show us what has happened today between the Nehawka and their enemies!"

So fires were stoked, food was cooked, and the Kaduza clothing and weapons were distributed throughout the village. Coyote asked for nothing. "If I needed clothing or weapons or food, I would take some," he said. "My clothing and weapons are obviously enough to bring me victory in battle and food from the field. I have come to the Nehawka only for a wife."

"Now you can show us in your song and dance how you won such triumph in your hunt and battle," said Full Quiver. He would have danced and sung and told the story himself if he had had any idea at all what had actually happened that afternoon. So, Coyote began his wild song:

> *I-you-we!*
> *I-you-we!*

and flailed around in his half dance, half stagger.
Many times he fell down as he whirled. Then he
got up and ran around the fire as if he were crazy.
He was so excited that he forgot the words he had
composed for the occasion, and instead sang only
his old song:

> *I-you-we!*
> *I-you-we!*

"Come join me in my dance, Full Quiver and all
my new hunting friends! Everyone sing my new
song! You, young girls, come dance so I can
choose a wife!"

The villagers could hardly keep from joining in
Coyote's dance. He had, after all, won a great victory for them, had saved many lives, and brought
back many goods and much food. It was now a
matter of Nehawka pride for them to join their
new friend, ally, and benefactor. To them he was
now a kinsman, though he danced like one of the
Contraries, those who do everything wrong and

backwards. So everyone in the village now began to sing Coyote's song:

> *I-you-we!*
> *I-you-we!*

and to jump and roll around the fire in imitation of his insane dance.

The din in Turtle Creek Village was unimaginable. The chaos was total. The usually restrained Nehawka crashed screaming into drying racks and fell into the fire, just like Coyote. They bumped into each other, cutting themselves and even breaking bones. They stepped on each other. They bloodied their noses. They cried out Coyote's song until they could sing no longer; they danced until they fell in exhaustion.

"I think that is about all the honoring we can do tonight, Coyote," said Full Quiver finally. "Why don't you choose a bride from among the beautiful Nehawka women so we can retire to our lodges for some rest after this long, glorious day?"

"Hmmm, well," said Coyote. He looked around at the ruins of the village. "Your clothing is tattered and your village is messy. You are sweaty and dirty. Some of you have fallen in the fire and your clothes are still smoking. Others are lying on the ground panting. Your women groan and rasp instead of saying soft words of courtship, as is proper. To my taste, you Nehawka are a poor and slovenly people. I appreciate your kind offer, but in all honesty I don't want to marry any of your women or be kin to any of you or live in such a poorly kept village. I really thought better of you when I first came here to visit."

And with that Coyote walked from the Turtle Creek Village back to his own village and his grandmother's lodge. "Where have you been, Coyote?" his grandmother asked him when he came into the lodge.

"Nowhere," Coyote said.

"And what were you doing all this time?"

"Nothing," he said.

Smoke took the pipe of tobacco Cut-by-Flint handed him, and a bowl of chokecherry soup from Cottonwood. No one said a word as Smoke finished his pipe, cleaned his bowl, and gathered up his gifts. He rose with the help of some of his nephews to go out into the cold night, where a light snow was now beginning to fall. As Uncle Smoke reached for the flap skin of the lodge to leave, a coyote's scream shattered the night's silence from the hills above Turtle Creek. Smoke turned and looked around at the people in the Big Belly Lodge. He raised his right forefinger and nodded knowingly.

"Uda," someone said from a dark family compartment in the lodge.

"Uda," said Uncle Smoke. "Uda."

GLOSSARY

Blue corn: Many different kinds of corn were cultivated by American Indians. Among the Omaha, a dark blue, sweet, very hard corn was common, and is still used today for ceremonial purposes.

Buffalo surround: On the two annual hunts, one in the summer and the second during the winter, hunters frequently surrounded and stampeded a small herd and killed animals in the ensuing confusion. Animals were often run off cliffs or into canyons where they could be easily butchered with little danger to the hunters.

Ceremonial: Modern Native Americans often have large gatherings, usually with many different tribes participating, celebrating Native American culture, dance, music, and religion. Parts of some ceremonials are private (for religious reasons) but other parts are open to the public.

Chokecherry (*Prunus virginiana*): Chokecherries are a common berry on the Plains; they are dark red clusters, almost black and very sour, growing on low bushes. Today they are often used for jellies. Plains Indians pounded them, pits and all, into thin cakes which were dried in the sun. Dried, they stored well and were used in meat soups during the winter. Tribes like the Omaha still use chokecherries in this manner. Chokecherries were also mixed in with animal suet and dried, powdered meat to make pemmican, a rich, easily kept food used primarily during winter months.

Clan: Plains Indian tribes were divided into clans that were usually, but not always, of hereditary membership. Each clan had its own rituals, songs, customs, taboos, dances, and secrets. They also had stories of the origins of their clan, often associated with an animal or natural phenomenon— like the bison or wolf, or the sky and the wind.

Contraries: Members of Plains tribes who were eccentric, perhaps even mad, and violated almost all tribal concepts of propriety and decorum. In our society we might ostracize such people, but within Indian tribes they were thought to be gifted with a special understanding of the Powers; they were therefore tolerated within tribal life and sometimes had specific roles in religious rituals.

Corkscrew grass (*Stipa spartea*): Corkscrew, or porcupine, grass seeds have long, sharp, stiff tails that twist and turn as the natural humidity in the air changes from day to day. The turning literally "corkscrews" the seeds into the ground, where they have a better chance of survival. Small bundles of this grass served Plains Indians as hairbrushes.

Cottonwood (*Populus deltoides*): The cottonwood is one of the most common trees of the Plains. Plains tribes often considered the cottonwood a sacred gift because it was so useful to them. The wood burns without sparking, which was very important in small tents and even the larger lodges; the leaves form the pattern of both moccasins and tipis; and the white "cotton" seed fluff that flies from the tree in the spring was chewed by Indian children as a gum.

Drying rack: Meat, especially buffalo meat, was preserved by drying and smoking. Women cut thin strips and slabs of meat and draped it on wooden racks over smoky fires, which kept insects and dogs away from it as well as giving it the kind of flavor that non-Indians still enjoy today in ham, sausage, and barbecues.

Flint: Plains Indians traveled great distances on foot to quarries where they could obtain flint, a glassy stone that could be chipped and shaped into very sharp tools and weapons.

Fry bread: Fry bread is a modern Native American food that came to them from the United States Army. Today it has been forgotten by white culture and is thought of as an Indian food. It is a baking powder dough fried in deep, hot lard. And it is delicious!

Gourd Dance: The Gourd Dance, or Tiapiah Society, is an elaborate set of dances and songs given to the Omaha by the Kiowa Tribe about twenty

years ago. It is quite different from other forms of
Omaha dance because the dancers move in
straight lines rather than independently. Each
dancer carries a "gourd" rattle, today usually made
of tin or aluminum.

Great Mysterious: Plains Indians often had no
name for their major god, only descriptive adjec-
tives, reflecting their belief that an understanding
of such cosmic powers is beyond the ability of
man. They knew there were great powers around
them but did not pretend to understand them.

Groundnuts (*Amphicarpa bracteata*): Groundnuts
taste a little like peanuts. They grow under-
ground, also like the peanut. Plains Indians and
even pioneers sometimes raided the nests of voles
and mice for their large stores of groundnuts.
These nuts are relatively rare today because of
modern agricultural methods.

Holy Hills: Most Plains Indians had geographical
sites that were considered sacred—hills, trees,
springs, or caves. Sacred ceremonies were con-
ducted at such sites, and sometimes it was
thought by Indians that spirits or animals used

the sites for their sacred purposes too. It was therefore extremely difficult for many tribes like the Pawnee, Oto, Ponca, or Cheyenne-Arapaho to be removed by treaty or force from their homelands because they felt (and often still feel) that the land was as much a part of their souls as their own flesh and blood.

Kaduza: A fictional enemy of the Nehawka.

Lakota: The true name of the Sioux.

Lodge: The Nehawka lodge in the stories is very much like the Omaha, Ponca, or Pawnee earth lodge: a large, round, domed construction about fifty feet across and set slightly into the ground. The lodge often had a long entry hall, usually facing toward the morning sun. A heavy timber framework was covered with poles and sticks and then earth and sod, resulting in a building suitable for housing thirty to fifty people with all their possessions.

Earth lodges were warm and comfortable; the Plains frontier sod house may have been modeled after them. During particularly bad weather and after the advent of the horse (which happened well after Uncle Smoke told his stories), horses could even be brought into a lodge for protection from the cold. In the center of the lodge was a fire pit, and directly over it in the ceiling was a smoke hole. With a little effort, young men could climb onto the top of an earth lodge for a better view of the village perimeter or events in the village.

Lodge compartment: Plains Indian earth lodges were divided into many compartments that served as private sleeping areas for family groups.

Lodge, muskrat: Muskrats (*Ondatra zibethica*) are common animals in the swamps and backwaters of Plains rivers, building large mud and stick domes, or lodges, that are easily visible. A common belief of Indians and white settlers alike is that the larger the muskrat lodges are in the autumn, the more severe the following winter will be.

Medicine bundle, Sacred bundle: Many Indian tribes had small packages of objects—stones, bird skins, seashells, bits of native metal—that had sacred meaning to them. These collections had power for individuals, clans, or tribes, and those who took care of them often needed to know special prayers or songs that permitted them to handle the very powerful objects without harm. *See also* **Sky Bundle.**

Moon: The Nehawka year was divided into "moons," occurrences of the full moon, each having a distinctive name. January, for example, was called "the moon of cracking cottonwoods" because during very hard winters on the Plains, it is sometimes cold enough that trees crack open with loud booms when the sap within them freezes solid. To the Nehawka, our July was "the moon the chokecherries turn black."

Nunwack: The Nehawka believed that a council of animals, the Nunwack, convened every winter in a cave along the high banks of the Missouri River to determine such things as the weather, the success or failure of crops, and the fate of tribes in the two annual buffalo hunts.

Orphan: Orphan is a traditional character in the

folklore of many Plains Indian tribes. He is a lone warrior in a setting where few could survive alone and, as a result, is considered a very powerful, very wise, very peculiar person.

Paint: The Nehawka decorated their faces, bodies, weapons, and household implements with paints made of minerals, plant saps and juices, charcoal, berries, and whatever else they could find that gave them the colors they admired.

Parfleche: A stiff, brightly painted rawhide envelope or box in which dried food, clothing, tools, and all sorts of personal and family possessions could be stored or carried.

Pawnee: The Pawnee are a nonfictional tribe that occupied what is now south-central Nebraska and north-central Kansas. They lived very much like the fictional Nehawka.

Pipe: Many Plains tribes traveled long distances to the pipestone quarries in what is now south-western Minnesota to quarry stone for pipes.

Pipestone is a soft, red stone that is easily carved and withstands the heat of burning tobacco. Modern Native Americans still quarry pipestone for pipes, sculpture, and ornaments.

Plains: There is a good deal of argument about the boundaries of America's Great Plains, mostly because there are no boundaries. Generally speaking, the Great Plains are the great grasslands in the middle of the continent, between the woodlands and prairies east of the Mississippi and the barren wastelands and mountains of the West. The Plains extend far to the south into Mexico, and as far north as the Canadian tundra.

Powers: This term is used for all of the mysterious and potent spiritual things that move above and beyond man—the Nunwack, the Thunderers, the Great Mysterious. Some tribes considered even Coyote and ghosts to be Powers.

Powwow: A modern celebration among many American Indian tribes. Among the Omaha, the annual powwow is held during the "waxing moon" in August and is a remnant of an ancient harvest festival. At any given powwow there are often very modern activities like baseball games and modern foods like cotton candy. On the other hand, there are traditional speeches, dances, songs, costumes, and customs, too. Most important, the powwow is a time for tribes, whose members may be scattered throughout the nation, to return to "the blanket" (the homeland and sacred landscape of the reservation) to renew friendships, embrace family, remember the old ways, and consider the future.

Rabbit, Jackrabbit: The rabbit referred to by the Nehawka is the jackrabbit (*Lepus californicus*), a very long-eared, long-legged hare that bounces across the Plains even today as if he were mounted on powerful springs. Rabbit was not simply an animal, however; like Coyote, Rabbit was a trickster—a person, a spirit, and an animal. In some stories, Coyote and Rabbit combine or exchange identities and you cannot tell whether you are hearing about Coyote or Rabbit, a man or an animal, or a spirit!

Robe: A robe is actually a blanket made of a tanned buffalo hide with the hair left on it. A well-tanned buffalo hide is warm and soft, and provided its owner with a fine bed, shelter from the wind during a hunt, and a good sitting place for a quick meal while traveling.

Sheephorn utensils: The large curved horns of the Rocky Mountain sheep (*Ovis canadensis*) were carved for ladles and bowls, but the trick was to hunt down one of the rare and elusive sheep. A household that had a sheephorn cup was fortunate indeed!

Sky Bundle: The Sky Bundle is a fictional collection of objects sacred to the Nehawka, especially to the Sky Clan of the Nehawka. The origin and history of the Sky Bundle are treated in detail in my book *Touching the Fire: Buffalo Dancers, the Sky Bundle, and Other Tales.*

Smokey River: This is the name often given to the Missouri River, presumably because of dust blown up from sand and mud bars in its wide bed.

Strike coup: Intertribal war was more a matter of pride for Plains Indians than inflicting physical harm on the enemy. A warrior gained much greater reputation and inflicted far greater humiliation on the enemy by striking him with a bow (*coup* is the French word for "blow") than by shooting him with an arrow or cutting him with a knife.

Sun Dance: Many Plains tribes still conduct the traditional summer dance celebrating the power and constancy of the sun in our lives. The dance takes many forms. It was made illegal in the United States for many years but was practiced secretly on many reservations. Today it is again legal.

Sweat, Sweat lodge: Even today Native Americans on the Plains use sweat lodges for physical and spiritual purification. Sweat lodges are small domed constructions of willow or cottonwood sticks covered with blankets. Stones are made very hot in a blazing fire outside and then are carried into the sweat lodge to a pit in the middle. Those who are taking the sweat sit in the low interior around the hot rocks. Water is poured onto the rocks, filling the interior with scalding steam.

Sometimes herbs like sage or sweet grass are put on the rocks as a fragrant addition to the steam. Many tribes use the context of the sweat lodge for prayers, songs, and blessing ceremonies.

Sweet grass (*Hierchloe odorata*): Sweet grass is still grown and braided by Plains Native Americans for use as a sachet in costume cases or even in homes. It smells like very delicate vanilla. Because it is hard to find, it is very expensive.

Thunderbird: The Thunderbird was a relatively minor mythic figure in Nehawka religion, a mysterious spirit-bird that brought storms, lightning, and thunder and could be very dangerous to any human who tried to seek its nest. Today the image of the Thunderbird is an important symbol in the Native American Church.

Thunderers: According to the Nehawka, the Thunderers were four important members of the Powers, spirits that guided the weather and other major natural phenomena like earthquakes, floods, grass fires, and death.

Tipi: The Nehawka, like many prairie Plains Indians, lived in permanent earth lodges during most of the year. On the biannual hunts, however, they carried tipis—conical skin tents. The tipi has many advantages. It is portable, large enough to house many people, tall enough to stand in, and able to accommodate a cooking fire. Today, canvas tipis are increasingly popular among Native Americans and non-Native Americans alike.

Tobacco: Plains Indians smoked Indian tobacco (*Nicotiana quadrivalvis*) in their pipestone pipes. The plant is rare on the Plains today, so modern tobacco has taken its place as an important part of Plains Indian culture and religion. Plains Indians believe that tobacco smoke carries prayers to the Powers.

Uda: "Good" in the Nehawka tongue.

Wasna: Wasna was dried and powdered meat, almost always buffalo meat. Sometimes it was mixed with crushed berries—wild grapes or chokecherries—and melted animal fat, in which case it was called "pemmican," a food especially favored during the cold months of the Plains winter. In camp, pemmican and wasna were eaten in soups, but they could also be eaten—out of parfleches or sacks—while traveling on the hunt or the warpath.

Wind Clan: *See* **Clan.**

Winter count: Nehawka years were measured not by numbers but by a name indicating some notable event that happened that year, usually during the winter. The year we call 1824 the Nehawka named "the winter the Smokey River fed the people," reflecting the memory of a herd of buffalo that froze into the Missouri River's ice and provided food for the Nehawka during a famine. The winter we call 1893 the Nehawka knew as "the winter the sky died," because it was that year that their sacred Sky Bundle left the tribe and was put in the care of an East Coast museum.

Young Woman Songs: For Plains tribes, almost every process of life, and certainly those points in the life of an individual or a tribe where things change—the seasons, the approach of manhood or womanhood, birth and death—had specific, elaborate rituals to mark the transition. Young Woman Songs were sung in the ritual marking the passage of a girl into womanhood.

ROGER WELSCH former professor of English and anthropology at the University of Nebraska, now writes full-time. His most recent work of adult fiction, *Touching the fire,* was a highly praised collection of short stories about the imaginary Nehawka tribe. Mr. Welsch, also an essayist for CBS's *Sunday Morning* with Charles Kuralt, and a columnist for *Natural History* magazine, is a longtime friend of the Omaha tribe of Nebraska. He was adopted by the Omaha in 1967 and given the name Tenuga Gahi, "Bull Buffalo Chief." *Uncle Smoke Stories* is his first book for young readers.